Masha and the Bear®
A Magical Holiday

Adapted by **Lauren Forte**
Based on the episode "Home Alone"
written by **Oleg Kuzovkov**

LITTLE, BROWN & COMPANY
LB kids

D1468298

© 2008–2017 Animaccord LTD. All trademarks are owned by Animaccord LTD.
www.mashabear.com

Cover design by Véronique Lefèvre Sweet.

Hachette Book Group supports the right to free expression and the value of copyright.
The purpose of copyright is to encourage writers and artists to produce the creative works
that enrich our culture.

The scanning, uploading, and distribution of this book without permission is a theft of the
author's intellectual property. If you would like permission to use material from the book
(other than for review purposes), please contact permissions@hbgusa.com.
Thank you for your support of the author's rights.

Little, Brown and Company
Hachette Book Group
1290 Avenue of the Americas, New York, NY 10104
Visit us at LBYR.com

First Edition: October 2017

LB kids is an imprint of Little, Brown and Company. The LB kids name and logo are
trademarks of Hachette Book Group, Inc.

The publisher is not responsible for websites (or their content) that are not owned by the publisher.

Library of Congress Control Number 2017941790

ISBNs: 978-0-316-43607-6 (pbk.), 978-0-316-43606-9 (ebook),
978-0-316-43610-6 (ebook), 978-0-316-43608-3 (ebook)

Printed in the United States of America

CW

10 9 8 7 6 5 4 3 2

It's the holiday season. Goat, Rosie, and Little Dog decorate a tree. They hang their favorite ornaments on the branches.

Masha runs outside to see. "Oh wow! I need to wake up the Bear!" she says. Her friend usually sleeps through the winter. But Masha doesn't care. She runs off toward his house.

At his house, the Bear is not sleeping. He is putting up decorations, too. He is very happy to spend a quiet holiday at home alone.

When Masha knocks on his door, he hides
everything. He pretends that he is in bed.

The Bear answers his door in pajamas. *"Shhhh,"* he says. The Bear fakes a giant yawn. He tries to get Masha to go back home, but she makes her way inside.

"Bear!" she calls when she sees his living room. "Are you not going to celebrate the holidays?" The Bear shakes his head and goes up to his bedroom.

Masha does not like that at all. "I will decorate this place in no time," she says. She searches for ornaments.

A top hat falls off the shelf and lands on her.

When Masha pops out of the hat, she is dressed like a clown. The top hat is magic!

Since Masha thinks the Bear is asleep,
she goes to tell the others. The Bear sneaks
downstairs to put up his decorations again.

Oh no! The Bear trips and drops everything! Pieces of decorations are all over the floor, and the tree is broken. What a mess! What is he going to do?

The Bear stands up his tree and puts bandages on the broken branches. He has one ornament left that did not break. Carefully, he puts it on the tree.

Masha walks past Sly Wolf and Silly Wolf as they decorate their tree. She tells them about the magic top hat. It starts to shake on her head!

She takes it off, and out pops a stuffed rabbit! Masha and the wolves are surprised. Masha gives the toy to the wolves as a present. "Merry Christmas!" she says.

When she walks by the chipmunks, something new happens. The hat shakes and out comes a nutcracker! The chipmunks love it.

The hat is granting wishes! Masha is happy to spread the holiday cheer.

When Masha returns home, she sees Little Dog, Goat, and Rosie. She shouts, "Look what I can do! *Abracadabra!*"

Boom! Masha has a brand-new snowmobile!

"Wow!" she says with a giggle.

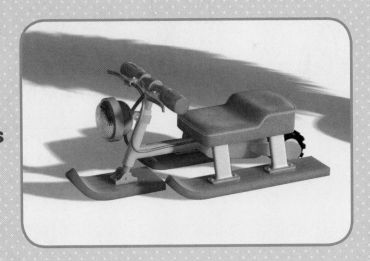

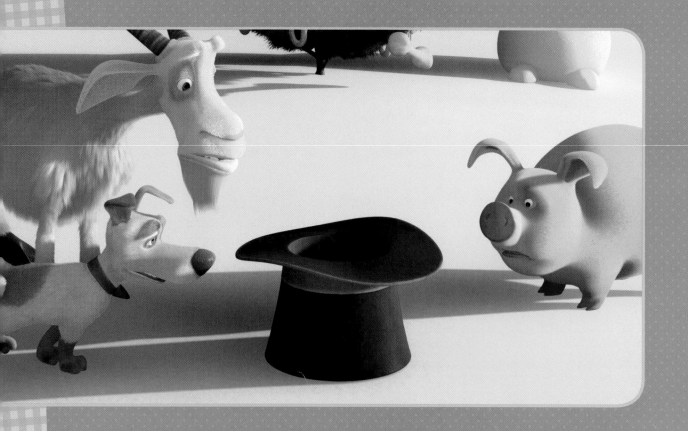

The others stare at the top hat. Will
something come out of the hat for them?

Zip! Zap! Zip! Out bursts a guitar, an accordion, and a tambourine! The animals can start their own band.

Later, the Bear finally realizes that spending
the holiday by himself might not be the best
idea. He feels lonely. He calls Masha, but she
isn't home.

Boom! Crash! Masha flies through the Bear's door on her new snowmobile, towing Rosie, Little Dog, and Goat behind her.

"Merry Christmas, Bear!" Masha cries, holding up a watering can that came out of the top hat for him.

The Bear uses the watering can, and his tree grows fuller! The branches are no longer broken.

Masha puts the hat on the floor. The hat's magic works again. Ornaments fly out of the hat and decorate the tree. It looks beautiful once more. "Woo-hoo!" cheers Masha. "It's the holidays again!"

The Bear picks up Masha and gives her a big hug. He is glad to have his friends over. He doesn't have to spend this holiday alone—not when he has Masha around.

© 2008- 2017 Animaccord LTD. All trademarks are owned by Animaccord LTD. www.mashabear.com